Is BROWN A Rainbow Color?

Illustrated by
Sameer Kassar

Written by: **Janesha Mohorn Beckford**

DEDICATION

To all the mothers and fathers who have lost a baby through miscarriage, stillbirth, or are still actively trying to build their families. I am no stranger to loss.

The storm is heavy, and this story is for you.

I see you.

I feel you.

Your rainbow is forming.

And my rainbow baby, D'Ari.

Once there was a brown girl named Ari.

Ari was intelligent, fun, and loved to paint.

One day while in art class, Ari decided to paint a rainbow.

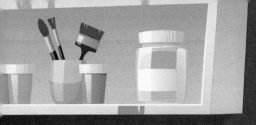

Ari's rainbow had the colors red, blue, green, yellow, and brown.

Ari decided to hang her

painting on the classroom's wall.

As Ari stared at her painting on the wall, a boy name Arnold walked up to Ari and said, "I do not like your rainbow painting."

"Why don't you like my rainbow?" Ari asked. Arnold replied,

"you put the color brown in your rainbow, and everyone knows brown is not a rainbow color."

and threw the picture in the trash.

Later that day, while Ari and her family ate dinner,

Ari asked, "mom, is brown a rainbow color?"

"Of course," Ari's mom replied.

Ari began to tell her mom what Arnold said about her rainbow painting at school.

To assure Ari that
brown is a
rainbow color,
Ari's mom said,

"I know brown is a rainbow color because you were my brown rainbow baby."

"What is a rainbow

"You know how
rainbows form

after a rainy day?" Ari's mom asked.
"Yes," Ari replied.

"A rainbow baby is a baby that comes after mommy and daddy have experienced a bad storm.

"A rainbow baby brings their parents joy and makes them smile like how you smile when you see a rainbow in the sky." Ari's mom replied.

"Wow! So, I am the rainbow?" Ari asked.
"Yes!" Ari's mom replied as they both giggled.

That night while Ari was lying in bed.
She thought about what her mom had told her.

The next day in art class, Ari repainted

her rainbow using only the color brown.

Mrs. Baker, the art teacher, asked each student to present their painting to the class.

When it was Ari's turn to present, she said, "This is my brown rainbow. A rainbow makes a person smile after a storm. My mommy said that I was her and my dad's rainbow. I made my parents smile after their storm. The rainbow represents me."

The class applauded Ari's presentation.

Ari then hung her picture on the classroom wall
and left it there.

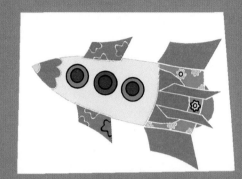

The End

Made in the USA
Las Vegas, NV
13 August 2021